Pop-Pops Amazing Bedtime Stories:

The Aviators Flight

James L. Capra

Illustrations by Blueberry Illustrations

ISBN: 978-1-7371167-0-7

This book is dedicated to my children, grandchildren, and to all the parents who inspire great imagination for young minds.

"Okay, kids, it's time to wash up and get ready for bed!" Grandma yelled from the kitchen.

4

Brayden and Faye made their way to the bathroom to brush their teeth. They were staying at their grandparents' house for the week while on summer vacation.

They finished brushing their teeth and were ready for bed. As they walked into the bedroom, they were excited to see an old red wagon in the corner of the room. They quickly scrambled into the wagon. Pop Pop and Grandma came into the room. Pop Pop chuckled and said, "That's the same

wagon that your mommy and her sisters and brothers played with before they went to bed each night. As a matter of fact, they would pretend that the wagon was magical and would take them on adventures around the world!"

7

The children's eyes lit up and all at once they asked, "Can we play for a little while longer?" Pop Pop and Grandma smiled and nodded as they walked out of the room. "Okay, fifteen more minutes, then prayers and bedtime!" Grandma said as she walked back toward the kitchen.

"Let's play a game," said Brayden. "Wait, I know what we can do," said Faye. "Let's fly to see our cousins Arthur and Avery for a visit." The children giggled as they sat up in the red wagon together and pretended to be in an airplane.

9

"Get ready for takeoff!" yelled Brayden.
Suddenly, the old red wagon began
to change itself. Brayden and Faye
looked all around it in surprise.

Brayden looked down and pushed
on a red button that was lit up
on the dashboard and all of a
sudden they found themselves
sitting in a real airplane.

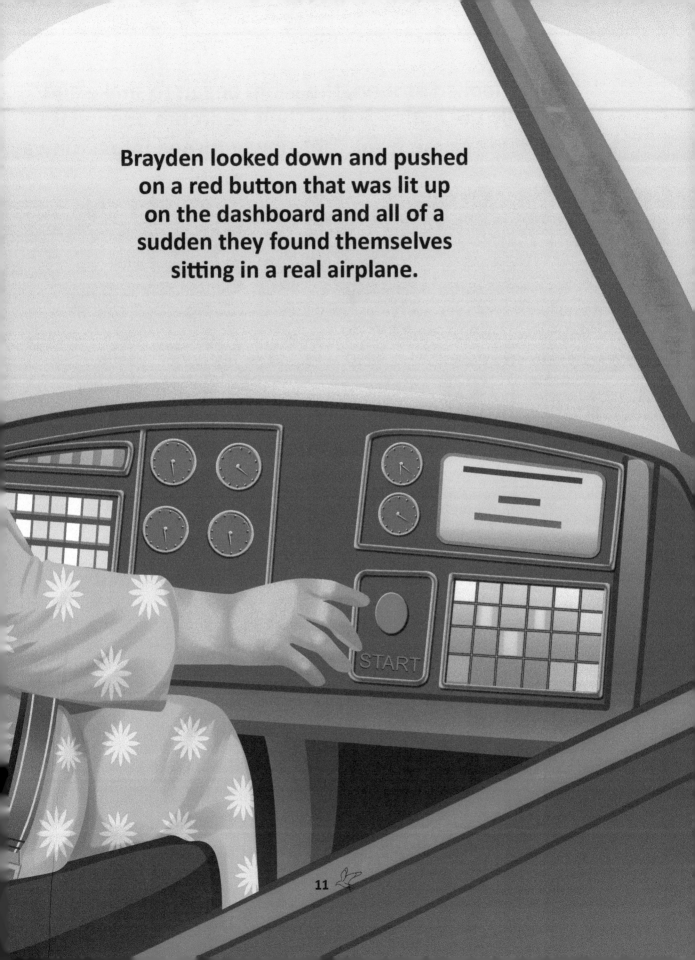

As they looked around, the room began to shake and magically the entire wall of their bedroom opened up to the outside as the front yard slowly turned into a runway.

Brayden and Faye looked at each other with amazement.
"Well, here we go!" cried Faye as she pushed the
throttle forward. The small plane rumbled
down the runway and took off into the sky.

Faye and Brayden were so excited to see all the flight instruments. They saw a blue flashing light on the screen which indicated where their cousins lived.

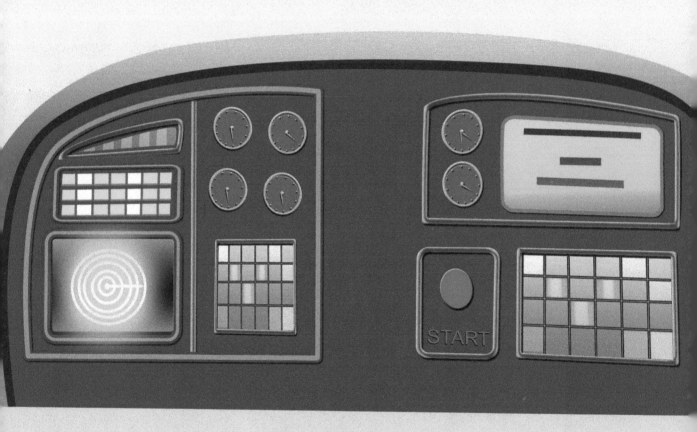

As Faye and Brayden turned the small plane, a flock of geese
ooked on with amazement seeing children flying an airplane!

Brayden looked at the instrument panel and called out, "Hey, what is that up ahead?" As they got closer to the object in the sky, Faye yelled, "Look out, it's a big eagle coming for us!" The eagle had mistaken the little plane and its young pilots as a yummy treat and tried to grab the plane with its powerful talons.

"Oh no, he grabbed our wing!" shouted Faye.

"I know what to do!" yelled Brayden. He quickly rocked the plane side to side while Faye pushed the throttle forward, making the plane fly faster and farther away from the big

eagle, which was now far behind them. "Wow, that was close!" shouted Brayden. "Now let's keep an eye out for Arthur and Avery!"

19

Racing across the landscape below, they soon
found themselves flying over their cousins' house.
They began to wave at them playing in the backyard.

When they landed, Brayden and Faye jumped out of the small airplane and ran to greet Arthur and Avery. Faye and Brayden shared with their cousins how the old red wagon found in the corner of Pop Pop's spare bedroom turned into an airplane when they decided to visit them. They all started to giggle with excitement and talked about their wild adventure.

All of a sudden, Brayden realized how late it was and shouted, "Faye, we need to get back to Grandma's house before she comes back into the bedroom!" Faye and Brayden squeezed and hugged Arthur and Avery goodbye and jumped back into the little plane. They raced back into the sky while waving to Arthur and Avery below.

23

They looked at the flashing blue light that showed them the way back to their grandparents' house. They turned the little plane in the right direction. They passed another airplane with surprised passengers peering out their windows.

As they flew closer to Grandma and Pop Pop's house, they began to see the runway appear on the front lawn. When they landed, the side of the house opened up once again to their bedroom.

As the little plane rolled into the bedroom, it quickly started to change back into the old red wagon just as they heard Pop Pop call out, "Okay, kids, it's time for bed!" Brayden and Faye jumped out of the wagon and scrambled into their beds and waited for Grandma to come into the bedroom and say prayers with them.

After prayers and being tucked into their beds, Grandma quietly said, "Good night, my little explorers," as she switched off the bedroom light. Looking out their bedroom window, Brayden and Faye saw a goose staring at them with a puzzled look on its face. Brayden smiled at the goose and with his finger over his mouth said, "Shh!"

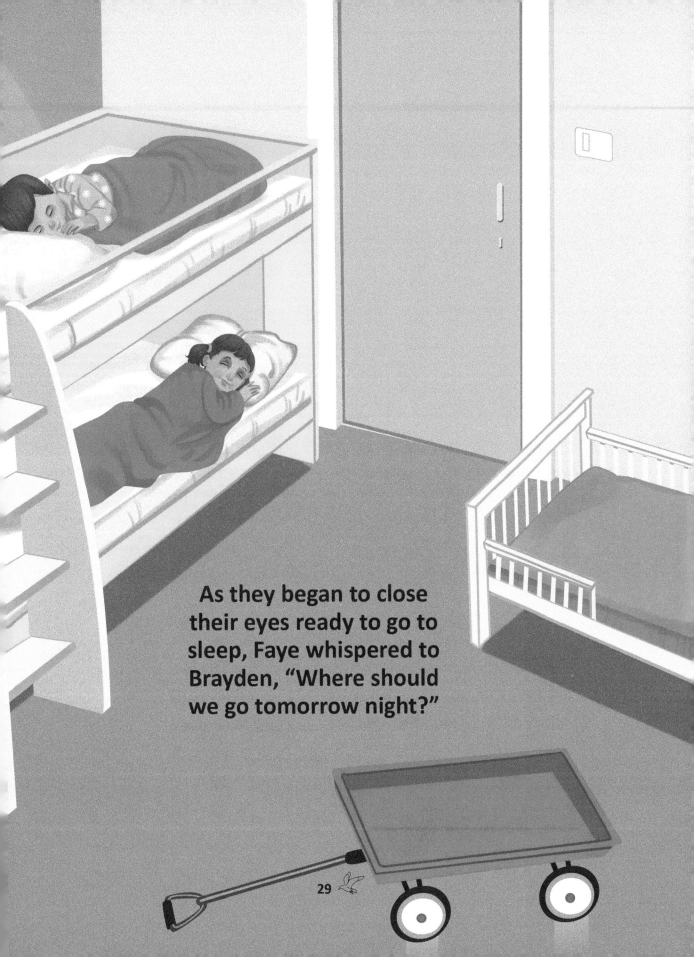

As they began to close their eyes ready to go to sleep, Faye whispered to Brayden, "Where should we go tomorrow night?"

29

James L Capra is an author, professional speaker, and the CEO of the Front Line Leadership Group located in North Texas. He has spent nearly four decades as a public servant both in military service and as a federal law enforcement officer. James has been married to his wife, Shelly, for over 38 years and they have raised six outstanding children who all continue to pursue their purpose in this life. He can be contacted via his website www.frontlineleadership.com.

CPSIA information can be obtained
at www.ICGtesting.com
Printed in the USA
LVHW071247070821
694775LV00003B/91